HOT WHEELS

THE MOBILE BROTHEL EROTICA

JACK RYDER

WARNING

This book contains sexually explicit scenes and adult language. It may be considered offensive to some readers. This book is for sale to adults ONLY.

Please store your files wisely where they cannot be accessed by underage readers.

* * * * * * * * * * * * * * * * * * * *

WANT FREE COPIES OF MY BOOKS?
Just visit my blog and download free copies of my books:
jack-ryder.awesomeauthors.org/jack-ryder

About the Publisher

4Fun Publishing, a member of **BLVNP Incorporated**, 340 S. Lemon #6200, Walnut CA 91789, info@blvnp.com / legal@blvnp.com
NOTE: Due to the highly emotional reaction of some people to works of erotic fiction, any email sent to the above address that contains foul language or religious references is automatically deleted by our anti-spam software and will not be seen. All other communications are welcome.

DISCLAIMER

Please don't be stupid and kill yourself. This book is a work of FICTION. Do not try any new sexual practice that you find in this book. It is fiction and not to be confused with reality. Neither the author nor the publisher or its associates assume any responsibility for any loss, injury, death or legal consequences resulting from acting on the contents in this book. Every character in this book is over 18 years of age. The author's opinions are not to be construed as the opinions of the publisher. The material in this book is for entertainment purposes ONLY. Enjoy.

Hot Wheels

The Mobile Brothel Erotica

By: Jack Ryder

© Jack Ryder 2015
ISBN: 978-1-68030-617-0

Chapter 1

It is still unbelievable to me how innocently this whole thing happened. It was a chance encounter motivated only by a genuine attempt to be of assistance to a very distraught young woman. I saw her at the edge of the parking area at the truck stop just off the highway at the edge of town. She was sitting on a concrete lot divider and was crying her heart out.

I'm not talking about a little sniffling. This poor little thing was sobbing uncontrollably with huge tears running down her cheeks and slobber running from her nose. I didn't really take a close look at her as I approached. I just felt I should see if there was something I could do to help her.

Seeing her so upset just made my heart feel broken for her and made me want to help her somehow.

"Are you okay, Hun?" I called to her as I approached her. Where she was seated, she was between my motor coach RV and an 18 wheeler that had parked in the next stall. "Are you hurt?

Or is there something I can do to help?" I added. When she lifted her head to look at me, I saw the most astonishing sapphire blue eyes I have ever seen. Even filled with tears they were the most beautiful eyes I have ever seen.

She took several ragged gasps of air as she tried to calm down enough to speak. "MY... sob, sob, sob... BOYFRIEND... sob, sob, sob... DUMPED me here." She then fell into another uncontrollable fit of sobbing. I sat down beside her and gently put my arm around her shoulder. "You're going to be okay, Hun." I said it softly. I was surprised when she leaned over and buried her face in my chest.

I decided it would be best to just let her cry herself out. I just held her gently as she blubbered for another five minutes or so. Her warm tears soaked through the front of my shirt and she seemed to be holding on to me firmer as she finally became quiet. "Everything is going to be okay," I told her softly. I used my free hand to brush some of her soggy hair away from her face.

I hadn't really had a good look at her when I approached her earlier. She had a young beautiful face with a little pixie nose and full pouty lips. And those gorgeous blue eyes which were now looking at me for the first time too. "Why don't you let me make you something to eat and we can talk about it," I suggested. I pointed at my RV when she looked a bit confused.

"I promise that I will be a perfect gentleman," I told her. "I just don't want to see you stuck out here where someone might try to harm you." It was just beginning to get dark out as she stood up. It was the first that I took notice of her tiny petite body. She was maybe 5 foot tall and just a tiny little thing. For the first time I had to consider how young she was. "I'm 19," she said it softly. She must have seen the concern on my face. As I glanced down at her, the top of her head barely made it up to my nipples.

"My name is Brad," I introduced myself as I bent down to pick up her duffel bag. I was surprised how heavy it was and wondered how this cute little thing would have ever been able to lug it by herself. "My name is Amy," she answered me. "Actually, I'll be 19 next month." She told me as we went up the steps into my motor coach.

"Wow...look at this," she gasped as she glanced around. I gave her a quick tour of my home on wheels. Then sat her at the kitchen table while I made us some chili dogs and french fries. "So, there is only one bed in here?" She asked it as I brought the food to the table. "Actually, the couch opens up into a queen size bed," I assured her. "If you need a place to sleep, I'd be happy let you have the bedroom and I could sleep out here," I told her.

I tried to keep my eyes from staring at her delightful little cone shaped tits as we ate our meal. But her nipples were erect and pressed against the thin fabric of her half halter top. The sort that just hangs below the breasts and leaves the entire tummy bare. I also noticed that the top button of her short cutoff jeans was unfastened. I could see just the top of her dark pubic hair poking above the open space.

As we ate dinner, Amy told me her tale of woe. She had left home at 18 because of a very abusive father. She had hooked up with a guy from her high school and he has been dragging her all over different states. She told me it was fun at first but had become a nightmare for her. Due to his drug addiction, she has had to sleep with many other men to make money to support his drug use. She confided that she had not objected at first, but now he has become nearly as abusive as her father, hitting her and slapping her quite regularly.

"Are all men like that, Brad?" she asked sadly. I told her that most men are NOT like that. "I have never raised my hand to a woman in my entire life," I informed her. "And I am three times your age." I regretted the last sentence the moment it came out of my mouth. Now, any possibility of getting in her pants has probably evaporated. "Really?" She sounded truly surprised. "You look a lot better than my father and he's 20 years younger than you."

Amy insisted on cleaning the dishes after we finished eating. My cock was fully erect as I sat on the couch and watched her. The shorts barely covered the top half of her ass cheeks. Each time she reached forward or bent over, I could see almost her entire ass and the thin bit of fabric that was wedged into her crack. My mind was racing with visions of yanking those shorts down and fucking her right there over the counter.

She was just rinsing out the big salad bowl and I noticed her secretly glance over at me. I averted her gaze to conceal that I was staring at her delicious little round ass. "Ooops," she giggled. Out of the corner of my eye, I saw her pour water from the bowl all down her front. Then she dropped the bowl to make it seem like an accident. "Oh shoot, I seem to have soaked myself," she said as she turned to face me.

"Ooooh Geeeeeeze," I moaned as I glanced at her directly. Her entire top was soaked through and the thin fabric was now transparent. I could very clearly see her perky cone shaped tits and her marvelous pink puffy nipples. The rest of the water had run down her belly and soaked her cutoff jeans. The wet crotch was wedged into her pussy causing a terrific camel toe effect. My dick began to throb as I watched the water on her belly dripping down into her pubic hair. I noticed that the second button of the jeans was now unfastened and I could see more of her mound.

"Oh, dear... I better clean that up," she giggled playfully. As she got down on her knees, her top moved forward exposing her wet little tits. The fabric wedged between her legs moved to the side exposing her ass pucker and pussy. "Oooh, Fuck Me," I whispered to myself as I gawked at her tight pink gash. I could feel precum oozing from my prick as I leaned forward just a bit.

You have to remember that in the small confines of the motor coach, she was only about four feet away from me. If I were to reach forward, I could easily pull her to me. I could easily reach out and touch her perfect little round ass. My hand was trembling as I reached down to rub on the painful erection in my pants. "You're enjoying the floor show," she laughed seductively as she glanced over and saw me touching my prick.

"Oh My God, Yes," I gasped loudly. "I'll show you my titties if you show me that," she offered. She grabbed the bottom edge of her top and pulled the top off over her head. "Your turn," she giggled. My hands were shaking violently as I fumbled to unbutton my 501 jeans. "Here, let me help," she offered as she reached up to pull my pants down when they were unfastened. "Oh, look at thaaaaaat," she purred as my 9 inch prick sprang out of my pants.

"I could play with that all night...if you invite me to stay," she whispered. "Oh Amy... Oh God Yes," I groaned as her tiny hand reached out to stroke my throbbing manhood. "Please stay with me, please stay," I moaned. Amy pushed my jeans down to my feet and then pulled them off. "Oooh, Fuck me," I bellowed as she took my dick head into her mouth.

The sight of Amy on her knees in those soaking wet cutoff jeans sucking my cock was the most arousing thing I had ever seen. "Yes, baby, yes!" I moaned as I reached down to stroke her soft shoulder length brown hair. Although she could only fit about half of my dick into her mouth, she used both hands to stroke up and down the shaft as she blew me. Gluck... Gluck... Gluck. She gagged a bit each time my dickhead poked into her throat a little.

My dick seemed to grow even more rigid as I watched huge strands of saliva drool down onto her perky little breasts. "You better stop or I'm gonna cum," I warned her as my legs started to vibrate and my balls began to swell with my load.

"That's okay...you can fuck me later," she kept stroking me with her hands as she lifted her head up to speak. "Ooooh Amy," I groaned when she took my dick back into her mouth and pressed even more of my cock into her throat. As her throat gripped my dick like a vice, I began to ejaculate. "Oh Geezus, Oh God... Oh God Yes," I screamed.

As my first wad of semen gushed into her throat, she gagged and a huge torrent of saliva and cum gushed out onto her tits. She pulled her head back so just the head was left in her mouth and she opened her mouth wide so I could see the second blast of jism spray into her mouth.

As she pulled my dick out of her mouth to show me the load inside, my third blast sprayed all over her chin and neck. I watched it ooze down onto her tits with the other mess as she closed her mouth and swallowed the load in her mouth. "That was...fucking incredible," I panted.

"I have a sister that lives in Phoenix," Amy advised me when she joined me in the bedroom after taking a shower. "I could keep you... really happy... if you could take me there." As I glanced up and down her sexy nubile body, there was no way on Earth I could possibly say no to her. "Ooh Fuck Yes," I groaned as she guided my dick into her drenched cunt.

Although I could easily make it to Phoenix in one day from Las Vegas, I told her I would need to stop in Flagstaff for business and it would take two days. "I'm in no hurry," she told me. I fucked her twice that night before we went to sleep and again in the morning before we started the trip south. When we stopped for lunch, she gave me a blow job before we took off to complete the drive to Flagstaff.

It thrilled me to see all the heads turning as we entered the diner at the hotel. I decided to get a room for the night so we could take a shower together and relax outside of the confined motor coach. Amy was wearing another pair of those indecent cutoff shorts and a white transparent blouse that tied in a knot just under her tits. "Your daughter should maybe put some clothes on," the middle aged waitress whispered as she handed us the menus.

I saw a mischievous smirk on Amy's face as she glanced up at the woman. "But then daddy wouldn't be able to see my titties." She smiled wickedly as the shocked expression grew on the waitresses face. "I usually wear nothing when we are at home." As the woman's expression turned to horror, Amy laid her hand on top of mine. "Daddy likes me to be naked... when I fuck him," she goaded the woman.

The poor woman's face was crimson red and her hand was shaking as she asked to take our order. "She's not my daughter," I informed her softly. "But I do like her naked when she fucks me." As she scowled at me, I winked at her. "Maybe you'd like to join us... we could do a mommy and daddy thing with her."

The waitress appeared completely disoriented as she left our table. Amy and I both chuckled as she bumped into several tables as she glanced back at us on her way to place the order in the kitchen window. I apologized for our playfulness when she returned with our meal. Then I tipped her very handsomely when we were ready to leave. "We will be in room 18 if you change your mind." I teased her as I handed her the money. I was certain that I saw a slight grin on her face as we left.

"Give it to me daddy... fill my pussy up," she wailed. I could feel her fingernails gripping at my shoulders as I plowed into her relentlessly. "Oh daddy... I'm gunna... gunna... cuuuuum." Her body began to jerk and spasm beneath me and I felt a hot gush of fluid spray from her gash. "Here it is baby... here it is," I grunted back. My dick exploded three times deep into her tight little pussy filling her hole till it oozed out of her even with my dick buried to the hilt.

"Oh Daaaaaady." It was that deep throaty moan again as her body quivered again. I released her legs and let them fall straight back onto the bed as I yanked my dick out of her. "That's my good little girl," I whispered as I reached down to pinch on one of her puffy nipples. "Maybe if you are a good girl... I'll let you ride me some more later," I taunted her.

I fucked Amy two more times that night and again in the morning before we made our way to Phoenix. Amy's sister told us to meet her at a nearest grocery store parking lot. She evidently had some misgivings about letting a stranger know where she lives. "Was he good to you?" she asked Amy when we climbed out of the motor coach. I could see her eyes roving up and own as she tried to figure out if I was a threat of some sort.

"Brad was wonderful," Amy cooed. "He was a perfect gentleman." I saw her mischievous grin as she said it. "You can be my daddy any time," she added playfully. She knew her sister Rose would have no idea what that meant. "And you can always be my good little girl," I chuckled my reply. I noticed that Rose was staring at my crotch now. I hadn't noticed that I got fully erect during our little banter, but she did.

Rose turned to Amy and told her to walk the two blocks home. "It will give you time to sort out what you plan to do about this mess you have created in your life," she told her. "I'll bring your duffel bag after I set things straight with... daddy Brad." She added with a smirk. Amy kissed me on the cheek before she left and secretly pressed a piece of paper into my hand with her cell phone number on it. "Call me if you come back this way," she whispered.

"What did you do to my little sister?" Rose growled at me. She was obviously the bigger version of Amy. Probably 5 foot 8 and ten years older. Her round 34C breasts strained against the front of her button down summer dress. But she had the same crystal blue eyes and pouty lips. The same light brown shoulder length hair. Her hour glass shape was very attractive. "Did you fuck her?" she rasped at me.

"Repeatedly!" I laughed my reply. Her head moved back as if I had just slapped her. "But that was after I treated her with kindness and respect. After we talked for hours and became close. And after she stripped naked and asked me to fuck her." I had crossed my arms in front of my chest as I answered her more completely. I didn't try to hide the raging boner in my jeans.

"Your little sister is wonderful," I told her softly. "Maybe you should try treating her with more love and kindness," I suggested. Rose suddenly looked confused as she reached into her purse to rummage for something. "Here... let me... pay you... for your trouble." She stammered it as she held out a one hundred dollar bill.

I sort of winced as I pushed her hand away. "That's not necessary," I snapped at her. "That would only prostitute the kindness I tried to achieve and spoil the very special time that we shared with each other." Her hand was trembling as she shoved the bill back into her purse. She very slowly walked to the door and then glanced back at me. Her eyes riveted to the bulge in my jeans.

SLAM. Between the time she slammed the door closed and traveled the 12 feet to where I was standing, Rose ripped her dress off and had her bra falling off as she flung herself into my arms. "Fuck me, Brad... fuck me like you fucked my sister," she moaned in my ear.

Without hesitating, I sat her on the couch and ripped her panties off. I dropped my pants and shoved my dick straight into her dripping cunt and fucked her brutally. Smack, smack, smack, smack. I pounded into her for several minutes. As I felt her vibrating into her climax, I yanked out and sprayed my cum all over her face and tits. "Ooooh Brad," she gasped.

As she dressed to go home, she promised to try to be a better sister for Amy.

#####

I decided to park the motor coach at the last truck stop on the way out of Phoenix. It would be better to get an early start for my next drive to Houston in the morning. I chose to make use of the truck stop shower since it was free with my fill-up of fuel, plus it would save my water supply a little longer. I grabbed a towel from the front counter and headed back to the shower area.

"Care for some company, Hun?" Although her voice startled me, it didn't really surprise me to see a hooker standing against the wall with one leg bent and her foot against the wall. The very tight mini dress she was wearing was cut so low that I could see most of her luscious brown tits.

The two cut out tear drop shaped holes in the front allowed you to see the bottom of her breasts and the lower one displayed her belly button all the way down to the an inch above her gash. It made it obvious she wasn't wearing panties.

Many of the lot hookers will hang out by the shower area to get away from the weather. Tonight it was just beginning to rain as I came in for my shower. "I'm only looking for enough to rent a room for the night." As she lowered her leg, she made sure I got a good look up her skirt at her bare cunt. "I'll make it worth your time," she whispered as she pulled her top open to flash her tits at me.

Her 38DD tits were a bit sagging. I would guess that she is in her mid 30's and probably of Hispanic origin. Her huge brown areolas were flat but her nipples looked like chocolate drops that needed to be sucked on. My dick was slowly swelling as I glanced up and down her full hour glass shaped body. "I think I might have a better offer." I reached out to hold her hand. It was nice to see a soft grin on her face.

As soon as we were in the shower room and locked the door, I handed Maria a $50. "This is for you, baby." I told her softly. "You already have a place to sleep tonight and I'll even make you dinner." As she leaned forward to kiss me, I unfastened my jeans and pushed them down to my knees. "I just have to fuck you in this nasty little dress." I groaned it as I pushed her against the closed door and slid my dick up into her cunt.

"Yes baby... fuck me... fuck me," she grunted. I pushed her top down and hungrily sucked on one of her nipples while I drove my cock up into her pussy. Bam, Bam, Bam, Bam. I was driving her ass back against the door so brutally it could easily be heard all the way down the hall. My legs quivered as I flooded her pussy with my seed. It did not concern me all that much that she did not get off. "I'll make your pussy happy in my RV," I told her as we showered together.

While I cooked us some burgers and potato cake patties, Maria found a robe in my closet so she could take off her dress. "You could just eat naked," I teased her. She had completely left the front of the robe open and her entire front was exposed to me. "I'll even take my clothes off too," I chuckled. "Just making myself at home," she giggled. "It feels nice... to be here with you." she added softly.

We shared a lovely evening together. We talked and watched TV off my satellite. She sat next to me and leaned up against me like a girlfriend would. "This feels really nice," she whispered in my ear during a commercial. She kissed me very tenderly on the side of my neck. When we finally went to bed, I held her hand as we went to the bedroom. I kissed her very passionately as I pushed the robe off her shoulders and let it fall to the floor.

"Now it's your turn, Hun," I told her softly as I crawled up between her legs and began to eat her pussy. "Oh Yes, Brad," she moaned. I felt her fingers tangle into my hair as she gently pushed my face further into her sex. "Oh God, that feels... so fucking good," she purred. I expertly darted my tongue in and out of her while I swirled my thumb around her clit. "Oh Brad," she moaned.

Her entire body was quivering by the time I scooted forward to mount her. "Oh Yes, Brad... yes," she groaned as I impaled her with my 9 inch prick. I fucked Maria very slowly. I pulled all the way out and then pressed all the way back in. Over and over very slowly as she trembled beneath me. I held myself up with my arms so I could look at her naked body and watch my dick sliding in and out of her gash.

"I'm gunna cum Brad... I'm gunna... Oh Yes... Oh My God... Yessss." I drove into her harder and faster as her body convulsed underneath me. Her head was thrashing back and forth on the pillow as I shoved all the way in one last time. "Oh Fuck Yes, Baby... Fuck Yes," I screamed as my dick ejaculated into her three times. Her body twitched again as she felt the heat of my seed flooding into her.

We slept very peacefully together that night. It felt nice to have her huge tits under my hand as we drifted off to sleep. In the morning, Maria climbed on my prick and fucked me like a cowgirl riding a bull before we got up. Then she cooked us pancakes for breakfast. "This has been the nicest night I have had in quite a while," she told me as we ate. Maria gave me her phone number before she left. She made me promise I would call her the next time I visit Phoenix. I now had three numbers scribbled on the back page of my address book. Amy, Rose and Maria. I wrote a side note indicating they all live in Phoenix.

Chapter 3

Cheri would be the next entry into my little black book. I saw her as I was pulling into the truck stop just outside of San Antonio. I decided to spend the night here rather than going all the way to Houston. It was just twilight as I pulled into the lot and I saw her hanging out near a large group of 18 wheelers on the back lot. Her long platinum blond hair caught my attention.

I made it a point to park in the nearest open spot to where she was standing. I also made sure that she saw me gawking at her. I gave her a slight boyish smile when she glanced over at me.

She seemed a bit furtive as our eyes met. I winked at her and shut off my ignition. She quickly glanced away but then her eyes wandered back to me.

She was an attractive woman that appeared to be in her early 40's. She had stunning legs that were displayed by the very short black tube dress she was wearing. There was an added slit up each side that allowed a great view of her creamy thighs. It also let you know she was not wearing any panties. Her full voluptuous breasts were held tightly in place by the dress but it showed a good bit of her ample cleavage and the fact that her nipples were hard and poking against the restraining fabric.

"Hello Hun," I called over to her when I stepped out of the motor coach. "I'm looking for someone to share dinner with," I told her as I walked slowly to her. "Dinner would be on me." I gave her a warm smile as I said it. "I would really love... some company for the evening." I added that so she would understand that I had more in mind that just eating. As she shifted her leg, I got a quick glance of her bare gash. I was hoping that she would accept my offer.

"I'm sorry... I'm sort of busy right now," she replied softly. I could see that she was glancing behind me at the three truckers that were coming towards us. "Maybe... Later... if I am free," she added. She was already making eyes at the men approaching us. "Okay Hun, I'll be in the diner... then I will be right here the rest of the night." I pointed at my motor coach.

I was about to walk away but thought of one last suggestion. "If you need to save the price of a room for tonight, I'd be happy to have you stay with me," I added softly so the other men could not hear." I slowly made my way to the diner. When I glanced back as I opened the door, I saw her climbing into a truck with one of the men. The other two men were waiting their turn.

I made it a point to sit at a booth next to the large glass window looking out into the parking area so I could watch. The first man climbed out of the truck after about ten minutes and a second man got into the truck just as I was served my meal. The second man stepped out of the truck twelve minutes later and was replaced by the third man.

I was sipping my coffee and waiting for my dessert when she came into the diner. "This seat taken?" she asked softly. Her hair was a bit disheveled and the top of her tube dress was now barely holding her tits inside. I could see glistening on her thighs caused by the lubrication of the condoms that had been inside of her.

"I was saving that seat for you," I answered her while I sat my coffee cup on the table. "My name is Brad," I added. Cheri told me her name and sat down next to me on the bench seat. I got a terrific look at her bare pussy as she slid onto the bench. She quickly reached down and pulled her dress down enough to cover up as the waitress approached. "Please bring Miss Cheri whatever she likes," I told the waitress.

Cheri got a wonderful grin on her face when I called her Miss Cheri. "You are quite a charmer," she chuckled as the waitress walked away. "I told you... I would really love to have some company for the night," I whispered. "So, I'm on my best behavior... is it working?" I gave her a boyish grin. "Jury is still out on that." Her eyes sort of twinkled as she said it. "But... you are certainly racking up the points."

Cheri ordered a chef's salad and I took my time eating my dessert so we would not be in a hurry. During our small talk, I confided that I was taking a yearlong vacation trek since I took an early retirement from a company that was downsizing. "You don't look old enough for retirement," she told me in between bites of her salad. "Now you are racking up the points," I teased her. It made me feel good that she giggled at that. She seemed fascinated by the thought of traveling around with no obligations and no planned destination.

The entire time that we were eating, I was able to see her pussy. Even when she saw that I was glancing down at her sex, she did not bother to pull her dress back down. "I'm glad you enjoy the view," she chuckled softly as we were waiting for the dinner tab. She even opened her legs a little further as she said it. "It's breathtaking," I teased her back. I asked Cheri if she would like to share a shower in the trucker area but she said that she would rather make use of the one in my motor coach.

"Is the offer to spend the night still open?" she asked softly as we left the diner. It was now dark outside as she wrapped her arms around my left arm. "I think I'd like that," she added. We made our way to the motor coach with her holding on to my arm. I saw several truckers watching us intently as I opened the door to let us in.

Before we stepped in, Cheri turned and pulled her top down exposing her tits to the staring men. "Sorry fellas, these are taken for tonight," she yelled over to them. She was giggling as she stepped up into the motor coach. "Now they know that they will have to look elsewhere if they want to get laid," she informed me with a smile. Her top was still pulled down. "My god you are sexy," I whispered. Her 38DD silicone jugs were magnificent.

As soon as she was in the living room area, she kicked off her sandals and wiggled out of her dress. After she used her hands to flatten it out, she laid the dress over the back of the couch and sat down completely naked. "Does this work?" she asked as she picked up the TV remote.

"Yep... just push the O--N button and use the arrow buttons to channel surf," I told her with a grin. "I have my own satellite," I informed her.

I took a very quick shower first since we could not both fit into my small shower stall comfortably. I made it a point to take a cold shower so she would have plenty of hot water for hers. "Look at you baby," she giggled when I came out of the bathroom naked. Even when my 9 inch dick is soft, it hangs down a good six inches. "There is no way that body is a minute older than 45," she told me as she gazed up and down my nude body.

Cheri stopped and kissed my cheek gently on her way to the shower. "This is going to be so fun," she whispered it in my ear as she reached back to squeeze my ass. "I hope you are up for an all-nighter," she giggled. As soon as she stepped into the shower, I went to the kitchen and took one of my blue Viagra pills. I wanted to be certain that I could have a good time tonight.

I poured us both a tumbler of brandy and lit some scented candles on the nightstand next to my queen size bed. I was happy that I changed the sheets after the night I spent with Amy.

"Wow...look at you, Hun," I gasped when Cheri came into the bedroom. She let the bath towel fall to the ground and just stood in the door for several moments. At 42 years old, Cheri is a very firm and voluptuous woman. She is a 38-28-36 bombshell. Her 38DD breasts are very firm since they are silicone enhanced. Her full hips offset the huge tits perfectly and her ass is firm and round. "My God, you are yummy," I whispered.

My dick was fully erect as she crawled onto the bed. "Oh Brad, that's delicious," she groaned as she wrapped her hand around my 9 inch prick. She seemed pleased that her hand barely made it all the way around my girth. "I took some Viagra," I whispered as I reached down to fondle her huge round tits. "We can play as long as you like," I advised.

"How long have you had this Lot Lizard Hotel?" She giggled it but there was a curious tone as well. I followed her gaze and saw the panties hanging on my bedroom door knob. The red thongs belonged to Amy and the black transparent bikini style were her sister Rose's. "I've had the RV for a couple of years," I told her softly. "But I have only been on the road for a week," I added.

"Don't like sleeping alone much, Huh?" she chuckled as she bent forward to lick around the crown of my prick. "Ooooh Geeeeezus," I gasped softly. "No... I don't," I replied after taking a deep breath. "Good," she giggled as she began to engulf my dick with her mouth. "Ooooooh yes, baby, yes," I purred. Her head was now very slowly bobbing up and down on my prick. It was the sort of blow job that makes your dick ache but not quite enough to get you off.

"You're not in any hurry, are you?" she giggled it as she dragged my dick back and forth across her face. "No... Oh God... No," I gasped weakly. Cheri already had my dick oozing seminal fluid as she moved up to drag my dick back and forth across her tits. The oozing precum left a little glistening trail as it seeped all over her cleavage. "You're such a tease," I gasped pathetically.

Cheri scooted up and sat on my thighs so my dick was wedged between her pussy lips. "This is just as much for my enjoyment," she whispered. I lifted my head to see her pussy lips wrapped around my dick as she began to grind back and forth on me. The sensation of her drenched cunt grinding on me was sensational.

I reached up to squeeze on both her big silicone tits as she rode me like an amusement ride. "You like those titties, don't you baby," she chuckled. "You can fuck them too if you want," she offered. "Later... Later... I want... to fuck you... first," I panted hoarsely. I was reaching over for the condom as she began to raise off my prick. "Do you have any diseases, baby?" she whispered.

When I told her no, she just laughed playfully. "Neither do I," she giggled as she guided my dick into her hole.

"Oh My God Brad, that feels so fucking good," she moaned. Cheri sat straight down till I was buried inside her drenched sex hole. She raised her hands to her head and was sort of pulling at her own hair as she began to hump back and forth on my prick. The expression on her face was absolute bliss while she slowly rocked back and forth. "Oh Fuck that's good," she moaned softly.

Cheri had exquisite muscle control. As she clenched and released her hold on my dick, it felt like a hot wet hand milking my prick. "Give it to me baby," she whispered in a deep husky voice. "Give your hot sticky seed." Her pussy was clenching and stroking my dick as she rocked faster. "Give it to me... Give it to me," she moaned. Squeak, squeak, squeak, squeak... the bed groaned from the force of her thrusts.

"Ooooh Cheri... God Yes... God Yes," I screamed. As my dick started to hose the inside of her cunt with my molten seed, she pressed down forcefully and vibrated as her climax overtook her.

"Yes baby...Yes...Yesss," she moaned as her body jerked and vibrated on top of mine. She sat there completely impaled on my prick for several moments as her climax reverberated through her again and again. "That was wonderful," she gasped softly as she fell forward to kiss me passionately.

We fucked two more times that night before we went to sleep together. I fucked her tits after giving her an orgasm with my fingers and tongue. Then I got her on her knees and fucked her like a dog while I pulled savagely on her hair from behind. It seemed like the harder I pulled on her hair, the wetter her pussy got. When she started to climax, I pressed my thumb slowly into her anus. She climaxed so hard that she wet herself.

Chapter 4

I heard Cheri talking on her cell phone in the living room area when I woke up in the morning. "Nobody has ever made me climax like that before," she was saying. "I have never wet myself like that before ever." She said it in a whispered tone. "I don't know if he'd be interested... but I'll sure do my best to convince him." After some giggles and a few whispered sentences, I heard Cheri coming back to the bedroom. I closed my eyes and acted like I was still asleep.

I felt her weight press down onto the bed and then the warmth of her naked body next to mine.

"Wake up sleepy head," she giggled softly in my ear. The softness of her breasts against my chest felt marvelous as she began to kiss the side of my neck. "Miss Cheri wants to play," she whispered as her hand went under the sheet to fondle my now swelling prick. "Oh, somebody else wants to play too." She said it playfully as my dick became rigid in her hand.

I opened my eyes as she pulled the sheet down and began to straddle my throbbing dick. "Gunna just have your way with me, Huh?" I teased her as I reached up to fondle her tits. "Should I stop," she said it just as she lowered herself onto my engorged prick.

"Oh My God, No," I gasped. After I buried my face in her tits for a few moments, I flipped her over on her back with my dick still buried inside. Smack, smack, smack... I pounded into her savagely shoving my dick as far as I could reach. "Oh My God Yes... Oh My God Yes," she grunted with each brutal thrust. I flooded her pussy with cum in less than five minutes.

"Good morning Hun," I chuckled as I pulled my dick out of her. She was still quivering as I rolled off of her. "Shall I cook you breakfast or should we eat at the diner?" I asked as I propped myself up on one elbow to gaze at her gorgeous naked body. "You really are gorgeous, Cheri." I reached over to softly pet her left breast. Her body shuddered as it created an aftershock climax for her.

When Cheri finally relaxed enough to speak again, she insisted that I should let her cook our breakfast so we could have some privacy. "I really am a pretty good cook," she insisted. I grinned at her and winked. "Prove it, baby," I teased. I gave her an old tank top from my dresser to wear while she cooked. It fit her like a short tank dress. Her tits pressed firmly against the thin fabric and the bottom of her ass cheeks just peeked out the back a bit. "Damn, you look sexy like that," I chuckled as I watched her in the kitchen.

"I have a little sister named Rhonda that lives in New Mexico," Cheri said it softly as she sat down with our plates of waffles. "When we spoke this morning, she had an interesting idea," she informed me. While we ate the wonderful golden waffles that Cheri had made, she told me of their proposed plan.

Roni, as she prefers to be called, had proposed that a rig like mine could travel around to truck stops and then some working girls like them could use the motor coach as a brothel on wheels. She had pointed out that during the winter or during any sort of bad weather it would be a real benefit since most of the other lot girls usually hate to come out when it's cold or any sort of inclement weather. She also pointed out the savings from not having to rent a couple of rooms.

I found the idea intriguing and agreed to talk to Roni. I have to tell you that Cheri was playing with my cock the entire time that I spoke with her little sister. I was very tempted to try this with them as Roni discussed the possible earning potential and agreed to an even three way split. My last concern was about what I would do with myself during the hours that they were busy with their hookups.

Roni suggested that we could still rent one room so we would all have a good shower and a bed we can all fuck our brains out after work. "Would you still... want to do that... afterward?" I was surprised by the suggestion. "I would insist on a good fuck after all the pencil dicks I have to deal with," she laughed. "Meeee tooooo," Cheri mumbled since she just took my dick into her mouth. "Ooooh God, Yes," I moaned as her mouth engulfed my entire prick. "Good... I'll see you when you get here," Roni giggled on the other end of the phone.

"Ooooh God Yes," I bellowed again as I flooded Cheri's mouth with my semen. "I take that as a yes," Cheri laughed while she wiped her mouth with the back of her hand. "How could I say no to an offer that good," I chuckled. There was still some cum oozing down her chin. "So, you won't have a problem with me banging your little sister," I taunted as I reached out to fondle one of her tits. "I'll insist on it," she chuckled back as she smacked my hand away from her breast. "But you better satisfy her like you did me," she said sternly. "I don't want to seem a liar," she giggled.

Cheri got off her knees. "Now, get dressed...we have some driving to do," she added. Roni was waiting for us at the front door of her two bedroom trailer home. Although the trailer park looked a bit seedy, her little home was clean and well kept. I noticed an older creepy looking fella in the trailer across from us was standing at his front door gawking over at us.

As I saw Roni standing in the doorway, I could see what he was drooling about. She was wearing black transparent bikini style panties and the matching transparent bikini style bra. Nothing else.

"Oh fuck me," I gasped as I reached the top of the steps. Roni is as different from Cheri as night and day. She is at least four inches taller which makes her 5 foot 10. Her perfect 36-24-36 body is very darkly tanned all over. Her 36C tits are like large cones that curve up slightly. Her shiny coal black hair hangs all the way down to the crack of her ass. Her emerald green eyes sparkle as she opens the door.

"That is my intention," she giggled her reply. I glanced up and down her gorgeous body as I paused to let Cheri enter the trailer first. "HEY... SHIT HEAD," Roni yelled over at the fellow that is staring at us as she yanked her top down to expose her breasts. "MY SISTER AND HER BOY FRIEND ARE GUNNA SUCK THESE ALL NIGHT." I heard a slight groan as he reached down to touch the throbbing bulge in his sweatpants.

"That will keep the pervert busy all night," she laughed wickedly. I could see that he already had his dick out and was stroking it as she closed the front door. "You enjoy torturing that man way too much," Cheri laughed. I did not bother to try to conceal the boner in my jeans as I dropped Cheri's duffel bag of clothes on the floor. "How can you two possibly be sisters?" I panted as I watched them passionately kiss each other.

"Step sisters... sort of," Roni responded after they finally quit sucking face with each other. "Her momma married my dad when she was eight and I was eighteen. Cheri added. "Then they divorced when Roni was eighteen and she came to live with me," Cheri grinned when she said it. "I only had one bed...we've never needed more since then." They both giggled at that. It was very arousing to watch them petting and fondling each other. There was such an intimate playfulness between them.

My cock was pounding inside my jeans as I approached them. I had a very deliberate plan in mind as I came up behind Roni. On the drive trip from San Antonio, Cheri had confided to me that Roni prefers rough sex. Because she sells sex for a living, she likes her lovers to rattle her cage. Cheri was grinning at me over Roni's shoulder.

SMACK... SMACK. "Awwwww," Roni yelled when I slapped each ass cheek once very hard. "Is it polite to ignore your guest?" I growled at her. SMACK... SMACK. Roni quivered as I slapped each cheek once again. Cheri smiled as she stepped back. "I'm gunna go and let you two get acquainted," she chuckled. "I'll be in the back bedroom putting on a show for the pervert next door." I could feel Roni trembling with arousal as I reached around from behind to roughly squeeze on her breasts. "I'm gunna have to teach your little sister some manners.

I used my free hand to rip her panties off. "Oh Yes, Brad... Oh My God Yes," Roni gasped softly. I dropped my pants and pulled her back to me as Cheri walked up the hallway to the back bedroom. "Ooooh My God, Brad," Roni moaned as I bent her over and rammed my dick straight into her saucy sex hole. "I told you," Cheri laughed as she stepped into her bedroom. SMACK, SMACK... I slapped her cheeks again with my dick buried inside of her. I felt a small gush of hot fluid run down my legs. "That's it baby, piss on me and make me yours," I laughed. SMACK, SMACK... More hot fluid gushed out. "Ooooh Yes," Roni groaned.

Squish, squish, squish... as I pounded into her gushing cunt, her juice squirted out and ran down our legs. I reached around front and smacked her right tit three times very fast and hard. Her nipple got so hard I thought it would burst. "Oh My God Yes... Take Me," Roni moaned in a deep primal voice. There was fluid pooling by our feet as I squeezed her right nipple and twisted it cruelly.

"OH FUCK YES... FUCK YES... FUCK YES." As she screamed out her orgasm, her body jerked and twisted. There was a huge gush of urine as she wet herself. "OH YES, OH YES, OH YES," she groaned as each wave of climax raced through her. The scent of her hot urine intoxicated me and I gripped her hips with a death grip as I exploded deep into her quivering cunt. "There it is baby... there it is," I grunted my reply. My legs vibrated as I emptied my seed into her.

I turned Roni around and kissed her forcefully after my dick fell out of her cum drenched pussy.

"That was... sensational," Roni moaned weakly. Her legs were so weak that I had to hold her in my arms to keep her from falling. "That's how you say hello," I whispered it in her ear as I gently fondled her wonderful ass. "Wait till you see what I can do in bed," I taunted her playfully.

We could faintly hear moaning coming from the back bedroom. When we opened the door to see what Cheri was up to, she was standing in front of the open window that faces the trailer across from us. She was completely naked and was drilling a huge dildo in and out of her cunt.

We could see the fella across the way masturbating while he watched the show that Cheri was giving him. He finally blew his load all over when Roni stepped behind her and fondled her tits and kissed on the side of her neck.

The three of us all took a shower together after eating the pizza that Roni called for. I fucked Cheri from behind while her step sister ate her pussy. It was thrilling to feel her tongue lapping at Cheri's hole while I was drilling in and out. When I felt the load racing for release, I pulled out of Cheri and Roni sucked the cum out of my knob right there between Cheri's thighs.

We decided to do a test run the next day before hitting the road. We discussed it at breakfast and I decided to not get a room. It was a remarkable experience for me as I sat in various out-of-the-way spots and watched them do their thing. It was wonderful to witness the cat and mouse seduction that would end with a man holding their hand on the way to the motor coach.

I could see the RV rocking slightly and then a few minutes later the man would leave alone. I watched this unfold a half a dozen times with each of the girls over the four hours. They each fucked six men and had made over twenty five hundred dollars including tips.

Chapter 5

The first three weeks flew by. The girls both screwed six or eight men each night between the hours of 8pm and midnight. Then the three of us would fuck like mating dogs till the wee hours of the morning and sleep in till noon or later. I must confess that I reveled in my new life with Cheri and her once step sister Roni.

We spent the first week in the Denver area. The air was thin in the mile high city but so crisp and fresh. The truckers seemed invigorated and the girls took full advantage of that. The second week we parked in a lot that was out near the airport outside of Salt Lake City. More than half the men they screwed that week were men in rental cars wanting to get laid before going off to a hotel alone. It was then that we understood that our rolling brothel was a fabulous idea.

We chose the truck stop nearest the Las Vegas airport for our third week. The girls worked from 4 pm till nearly two in the morning. Even when they called it a day, they could easily have screwed many more men. There was a huge pile of money that we shoved into the secret floor safe under the master bed that first night. It was the same over the next four days.

Although the money in Vegas had been very good, both of the girls were exhausted by the end of that fifth evening. They had earned more money than the two weeks prior. But they were both so worn out by the end of each night that we had not played together since we arrived here. I made a decision when we got up that Saturday morning to take a break for a couple of days.

Cheri and Roni were ecstatic when I told them I had rented us a suite at one of the famous casinos downtown. I made the call before they woke up and had booked the room till noon on Monday. They dragged me back to the bedroom and took turns fucking me till they had me completely spent. It was wonderful to watch them both scurrying around like excited little girls as they got themselves ready to go check into our suite.

The first thing they did after check in was to visit the hotel salon to get all dolled up. Then they did some shopping at a local lingerie store where they bought several new outfits and new bras and panties. They were like giggly little girls with new Christmas presents when they got back to the room. It made me feel really good to see them both so relaxed and joyful. After lots of giggling and whispering in the locked bathroom, they came out to give me a special thank you.

Because they know what a thrill it is for me to watch them together, they decided to put on a very special little private show for me. They were wearing identical bright red transparent baby doll nighties. They started by turning on some music and dancing together very seductively. Just like you would see at a good strip bar when the girls dance around and rub all over each other. My dick was hard as a rock just watching them bump and grind on each other.

By the time the third song started, they were very provocatively stripping each other while they took turns fondling each other and nibbling on each other's nipples. Once they were down to just their matching transparent panties, they made a big production out of rubbing each other between the legs. I pushed my jeans down and began to play with myself as they both began to moan softly.

I felt a huge gush of seminal fluid as I watched Roni pull Cheri down onto the floor and then started to rub her face in Cheri's crotch. Within a few moments, Cheri's panties were saturated with the fluids of her arousal. "Oooh Geeeeezus, Yes," Cheri gasped when Roni pulled her panties to the side and shoved her tongue deep into her sloppy wet sex hole. Within a few more moments, they both had their panties off and were going at it in a 69 position.

I made it a point to only stroke myself very gently. Although I wanted to climax, I also wanted my show to last as long as possible. I was rewarded when they pulled me down onto the floor and took turns fucking me after they had got each other off in front of me. We then soaked in the hot tub Jacuzzi and called for an early dinner from room service. Although none of us were into gambling, we did want to go down and play the one arm bandits for a while.

We had been down on the main floor for about an hour. Cheri was seated to my left and Roni was to my right on the very end of the row of slots. They had worn identical outfits of shredded jeans which had huge open slices on the thighs and also in the back. The ones in the front allowed a nice view of their thighs almost up to the gash. In the back, you could practically see both ass cheeks. They had both also worn extremely tight tube tops. Although the fabric covered the breasts, they were so tight that you could see the entire shape of their tits pressed against the top.

There had been several men that came up to Roni and asked her for a date. She politely informed each man that she was simply enjoying a vacation with her sister. I saw him as he walked over towards us. Perfect suit and tie, perfect sun tan and perfect smile. "Could I solicit some of your time?" He asked Roni quietly. Roni smiled sweetly and told him he was mistaken.

"I am here to enjoy a vacation with my sister and I certainly have no interest in being solicited," she told him.

"Let me... start over." He sort of chuckled it. "I would love to spend some time with you... and I just want to... make sure you are compensated... for the interruption from your... family time." As he turned his head, we could see the ear bud in his ear. "That still sounds like you are soliciting me Mr. Security man," Roni sounded annoyed now. She scooted over closer to me and Cheri.

"Oooh... No, No, No," he chuckled. He took a quick look over his shoulder and pulled the bud out of his ear. "I am Sam Jones... the operations CEO." He confided. "I'm off duty... and I would love to have your attention... for the evening." He said it very softly and he sounded sincere. Roni reached up and gently petted his arm. "To be perfectly clear... you are asking me for a date and that is all?" she inquired.

After Sam convinced her that all he wanted was to spend some time with her, she accepted his offer. "Don't wait up mom and dad," she teased us as she wrapped her arm around his. "I will take very good care of her... mom and dad," he chuckled. I saw him put his ear bud into his pocket as they were walking away. I had to laugh when I saw Roni gently fondle his ass while they were waiting for the private elevator that goes directly to the penthouse.

Cheri had a goofy sort of look on her face when I turned back around to face her. "Alone for the first time in three weeks," she giggled softly. "Why don't we go back to our room?" She said it softly as she reached over and gently touched my leg. "I got a surprise for you today." She still had that goofy look on her face.

Cheri kissed me passionately and rubbed her body against mine in the elevator up to the 14th floor. Then she made me wait out on the balcony while she got her surprise ready for me. "Oh baby... look at you," I exclaimed when she stepped out on the balcony to join me.

She had changed into a very sexy teddy type nightie. It was light shade of teal with white ribbon around the neck and laced down the front. It had a snap open crotch. "I want you to fuck me right here on this balcony," she whispered as she began to unbutton the dress shirt I was wearing. As soon as she had me stripped naked, she pushed me down onto the chaise lounge.

"Now... let's put on a show," she chuckled as she crawled up between my legs and took my dick into her mouth. As she began to suck up and down my swollen prick, I noticed that there were several men that could see us from their balconies in the hotel across the street from us. By the time Cheri scooted up and mounted me, there were at least a dozen men watching us. Several of them had binoculars and two of the men appeared to be recording us with large hand held video cameras.

It was a remarkably arousing to see the men jerking off as they watched Cheri humping me. I pulled her nightie off over her head then flipped her onto her back. "Yes baby, fuck me," she moaned as I drove my dick as far into her as it could go. Squeak, squeak, squeak... the lounge chair groaned in protest as I pounded into Cheri so forcefully that chair was sliding back across the patio.

"Fuck Me... Fuck me... Make me yours," she screamed. I'm sure the men across from us could hear her. CRASH... the lounge chair collapsed. "Uuuumffff," Cheri gasped as my weight pushed the air out of her lungs. As I drew back to get off her, she wrapped her legs around my waist. "Don't you stop... don't you stop," she grunted at me.

Bam, Bam, Bam, Bam. The chair crashed against the floor as I pounded into her harder and harder. I saw each of the men across the way jerk and shudder as they shot their creamy loads all over their balcony walls. "Yes baby... give it to me... give it to me," Cheri wailed as she felt my semen flooding into her quivering womb. I felt her vibrate beneath me as she climaxed too.

I could hear clapping and whistles as we went back into our room. "You know, we were being recorded," I told her as we shut the curtain inside the room. "It better go viral or I'll be offended," Cheri laughed her reply. I was suddenly startled by the sound of giggling. I was astounded when I turned around and saw Amy and Rose both sitting on the queen sized bed. "How in the world?" I gasped in disbelief.

While Amy and Rose gave me hugs and kisses. Cheri told me that they had called my cell phone early this morning while I was sleeping soundly. They had wanted to ask if they could join me on my trip because they were both out of work. Rose had lost her job as a legal assistant because she objected to her boss's sexual advances. Amy had been scared off from the local truck stop because some older girls assaulted her because she was taking too much of their business. "I told you I had a surprise," Cheri laughed cheerfully.

"Cheri and I are going next door," Amy blurted out as she stood up. "We reserved the room this afternoon," she added. "Enjoy your surprise baby," Cheri whispered in my ear as she bent forward to kiss my cheek. "You two have a lot to catch up on," she giggled as she and Amy went through the door between the two rooms.

"It's so nice to see you again, Brad." Rose spoke almost bashfully as she stared at my naked body. Although she was dressed much more provocatively than when I first met her, she was still a little on the bashful side. "Are you sure... you can do this?" I asked her as I reached over to pet her left leg. I noticed that her legs started to spread open more as soon as I touched her.

"I can do anything... as long... as I can be with you," she moaned softly. I had moved my hand up inside her mini skirt to her drenched panties. She trembled as I dragged a finger up her slit.

"The men will want to fuck you like a whore and tell you what a slut you are."

"Oooh My God, Yes," she moaned as I pulled her panties to the side and shoved two fingers into her sex. "They will want you to suck their dirty little dicks and tell them how manly they are."

"Oooooh Yes!" Her entire body quivered when I wiggled my fingers inside her hole.

"Some men will be rough with you." I shoved her back and rolled her on her stomach. "They will just take you however they please." "Oooooh My God," she moaned as I ripped her panties down to her ankles. "Oooooh Fuck Me," she gasped as I got on top of her and slipped my cock straight up her ass. "Oooh Braaaaaaaad." It was a deep husky primal sort of moan.

Slap, slap, slap, slap. My belly bounced against her ass cheeks as I pounded into her brutally.

The tightness of her virgin asshole was exquisite. "Ugh, Ugh, Ugh, Ugh," Rose grunted loudly as I drove into her over and over. "Are you sure you want this, Rose?" I growled into her ear.

"Take Me Brad.... Take Me," she moaned throatily. I was surprised when she began to vibrate into climax. As I flooded her ass with my load of cum, she wet herself right there on the bed. While we rested afterward, she told me that Cheri had told her that she would share me with her. "We are both in love with you," she whispered.

Rose purchased a motor coach with the money she earned from selling her home in Phoenix. It is identical to mine except it is a year newer. Cheri, Rose and I travel in my motor coach and Amy stays with Roni in the newer RV. The two of them seemed to really hit it off from the moment they met. They love traveling together and adore sleeping together. I cherish the unique relationship that has developed with Cheri, Rose and me. You may see our identical motor homes if you travel in the four corner state areas. The matching bumper stickers on the back read: Lizard Lot Hotel 1 and Lizard Lot Hotel 2.

~~The End~~

Here is a sample from another story you may enjoy:

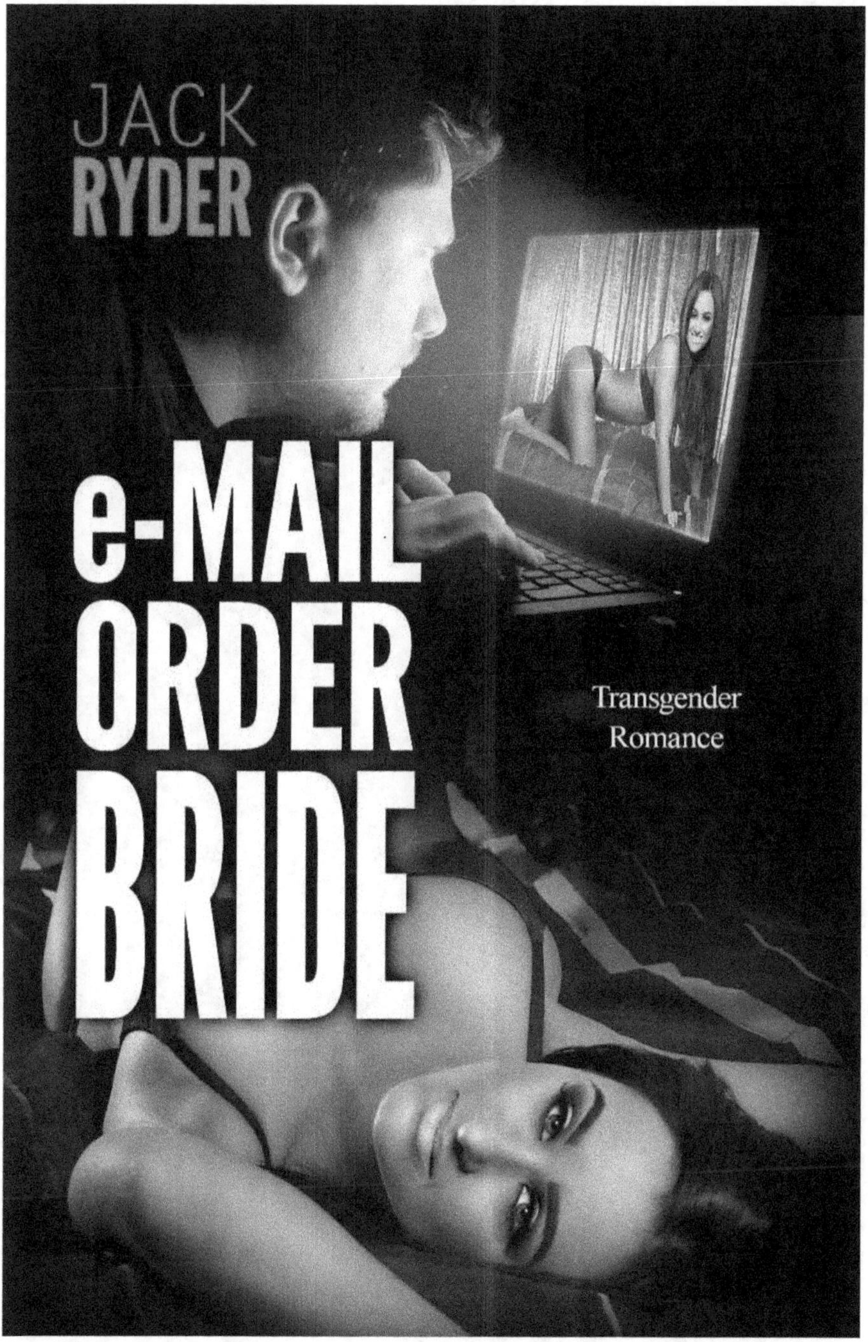
JACK
RYDER
e-MAIL
ORDER
BRIDE
Transgender
Romance

Seatac was a mad house at 9pm on a Friday night. I was glad that I had left early so I had plenty of time to deal with the sports traffic on I-5 due to the Mariners Game. Then I had to deal with the security checks to make my way to the proper air terminal gate for Sam's arrival. I made it to the gate with ten minutes to spare. I felt an overwhelming giddiness as I watched her airplane pull up to the loading dock.

"Ooooh, Fuck me," I gasped beneath my breath as I saw her coming down the ramp. She was wearing a white tube dress that fit her like a second skin. It was so short that I could see the bottom inch of her white panties as she walked towards me. She was wearing a big round black hat and her long black hair was in a tight braided ponytail. She had huge dark sunglasses on and was smiling broadly as she got closer and closer. Her long muscular legs looked fabulous.

"You are even more gorgeous in person," she told me in that wonderfully husky voice as she bent forward to kiss one cheek and then the other.

"Oh Sam...You look gorgeous," I groaned my reply. It thrilled me to see all the heads turning as we made our way to the baggage claim to get her luggage. And even more when she reached down to hold my hand as we waited at the turnstile.

"Ha-ha-ha-ha, I should have guessed that you would have a Hummer," Sam giggled when I pointed out my forest green Humvee.

"It was my divorce present to myself," I informed her as I opened the passenger door. "And my cabin in the hills was the other." My dick wiggled as she swung her legs into the vehicle. I got a quick glance of her white panties and a great look down the top of her dress at her tits. Her nipples were just as hard as last night.

"I have something to tell you before we get to the hotel." She said it very softly as we were pulling out of the parking garage. "I make porn movies, Bobby...I am a porn Queen in Russia."

I glanced over at her and she was gazing at me intently. "Wow, Sam...How did I ever get so lucky?" My voice sort of trembled a bit. "I'm even more amazed that you have an interest in me now."

I felt her hand rest gently on my thigh as I turned my attention back to driving the vehicle. "I think that I may be the lucky one," she whispered it softly. "I came here to see you because there is something I need to show you." She said it so softly that I could barely hear her. "I have a feeling about you...that it will be okay." Her hand gently brushed up and down my thigh. I could feel my dick throbbing in my jeans. "You have no idea how much I hope I am right," she added.

I couldn't keep my eyes off of Sam while she was checking in at the hotel. Neither could any of the other men in the front lobby area. By the time we made it to the elevator, several of the bell hops and a couple of the men from the lobby had asked Sam for her autograph. Except they knew her by the name Samantha Bone.

I could tell that Sam was a bit annoyed and upset as the elevator started to rise towards the penthouse suite. "It bothers me that all those men knew who I am and have seen me naked," she whispered it softly. "But you haven't yet." She sort of hung her head as she finished.

I reached over and held her hand gently. "I'm sure that whatever you are worrying about will be okay," I told her as I squeezed her hand. "I've been told that I am a fairly progressive sort of man." I chuckled.

Sam turned to face me and gave me a half smile. "I certainly hope you are, Hun," she answered me.

As soon as were in the penthouse suite, Sam kicked off her white heels and tossed her black hat onto the easy chair near the kitchen. She sat her sunglasses on the counter then reached up to grab a bottle of vodka from the top cabinet.

"Oh Geezus," I gasped as I gazed at her ass sticking out under her tight dress as it pulled up in back.

Sam poured the vodka into two 4 oz. tumblers then carried them and the bottle back into the living room. "Sit on the couch and be comfortable," she told me as she handed me one of the drinks. After she slammed down her entire drink, she pointed to mine. "Bottoms up...Hun," she giggled. As soon as I swallowed mine down, she refilled both tumblers and then stepped back about two feet from the couch.

"Moment of truth," she chuckled softly. Standing directly in front of me, she slowly pulled down the top of her tight dress until her tits were fully exposed to me. "Oooh Sam," I gasped. I could feel my pecker swelling in my jeans as I glanced at her gorgeous tits.

"The reason I didn't tell you about the porn movies is that I was afraid that you might ask me what sort of porn." She said it as she wiggled her dress down to her feet and kicked it off. I could now see that she wasn't wearing white panties, it was a white bikini bottom.

"You are so gorgeous, Sam," I moaned as I gawked at her beautiful body.

"Yes...but you haven't seen all of me yet," she whispered as she pulled the strings on her bikini and it fell off.

What she had on underneath the bikini I had never seen before. It was like a thong. But not quite a thong. It was a small fabric cup sort of thing with a thong strap in the center that went up the crack of her ass. There was a thick string that wrapped around her waist and tied to the center fabric in back. "This is what you haven't seen," she said it timidly as she reached behind to untie the string.

As the tiny cup fell to the floor, I was stunned and exhilarated at the same instant. My eyes were riveted between her legs at the perfect six inch flaccid cock. "Oooh Sam," I whispered. "That is so...extraordinary." I could feel my dick throbbing.

"It's....okay?" Sam cooed as her eyes lifted up to peer into mine.

"Oh Sam, it's better than okay...it is...wonderful! I want to feel it get hard in my hand this first time," I whispered as I reached forward to gently fondle her perfect six inch dick...

If you enjoyed this sample then look for <u>e-Mail Order Bride</u>.

Also by this Author:

The Handyman Seduction

The Beer Bust Scandal

Scandalous Emotion

Intimate Relation

The Seduction of Kimi

Erotic Goes Hi-Tech

One at a Time

The Wizard Casey's Coven

The Inn Keeper's Wizard: When Love and Magic
Collide

Trailer Trash Payback

Queer Intentions

Zoe's Fun House

Public Display

Test Drive

Breaking the Bonds

Trailer Trash Payback

The Hero's Welcome

The Twenty-Eight Day Cure

The Cougar Club

The Wife Swap

In Love with a Cougar

Stella for Christmas

The Long Ride Home

A Shot at Love

My Swedish Greta

The Second Honeymoon

Candy's Playmate

Sara's House of Hands

Loving My Sitter

His Wife and Her Husband

Bi-Curious Couple

Take Three, Mr. Writer

Hired For Their Pleasure

Blackmailed Nanny

The Daring Doppelgangers

Serving the Therapist

Corrupting the Choir Boy

The Cheating Game

Tempted and Tamed

E-Mail Order Bride

All Night Arcade

The Step Monster MILF

Storm Warning

About the Author

Jack Ryder LOVES everything there is about sex!

When he is not involved with his "swinger" friends, enjoying a steamy threesome, or being part of a raunchy "gang bang", you can find him on first class planes, trains, and cruise ships. Traveling seems to be the BEST way to finding new and interesting sexmates for him. Sexmates. Plural. He lives with the saying "The More, The Merrier!"

He owns a successful business in New York. He writes as a hobby and also as sort of documentation of his mind-blowing sexcapades over the years. He is presently roaming around the streets of Manhattan but can be anywhere in the world too, since he travels often. So, beware! You just might be his next mate.

*"The most fun thing I enjoy when writing my stories is trying to figure out which is fantasy and which was memory. ENJOY! (Preferably with a friend. *wink*) " -Jack Ryder-*

WANT FREE COPIES OF MY BOOKS?
Just visit my blog and download free copies of my books:
jack-ryder.awesomeauthors.org/jack-ryder